D1135074

OTHER BOOKS IN THE
LITTLE POLAR BEAR SERIES

Ahoy There, Little Polar Bear
Little Polar Bear Finds a Friend
Little Polar Bear, Take Me Home!
Little Polar Bear and the Brave Little Hare
Little Polar Bear and the Husky Pup

First mini-book edition published in the United States, Great Britain,
Canada, Australia, and New Zealand in 2000 by North-South Books,
an imprint of Nord-Süd Verlag AG, Gossau Zürich, Switzerland.

ISBN 0-7358-1273-X
1 3 5 7 9 10 8 6 4 2
Printed in Italy

Little
Polar Bear

Written and Illustrated by
Hans de Beer

North-South Books
New York / London

It was a big day for Lars. He was going with his father on his first hunting trip.

Lars was white all over, just like his father. In fact, at the North Pole where Lars lived everything was white because it was covered in ice and snow.

Lars's father showed him how to do all kinds of things: follow tracks, swim, and dive. He talked and talked and Lars listened silently, paying close attention. Once his father disappeared underwater and stayed so long Lars began to worry. But when his father finally reappeared, he had a big fish for supper.

When it was time to go to sleep Lars's father said, "Make a big pile of snow to protect yourself from the wind, like I do."

Lars was proud of his pile, but also very tired. He quickly fell asleep, just like his father.

But during the night the ice began to crack. The piece where Lars was lying broke off.

When Lars woke up it was morning. He was all alone
in the middle of the sea. It was getting warmer and warmer
and the piece of ice and Lars's pile of snow were getting
smaller and smaller.

When the ice was almost completely melted Lars saw a big barrel drifting by. Luckily Lars was able to reach the barrel and climb on top of it.

Then a storm began to rage. As Lars clung to his bobbing barrel he missed his father and his pile of snow more and more.

After the storm Lars drifted on the sea for a long time. At last he saw land but could not see any snow or ice. Almost everything was green and the sun was very warm. Lars carefully slid off the barrel and stepped onto the beach.

The beach was hot and yellow. It burned Lars's paws.
He ran to a river nearby. But just as he was about to
plunge in, a very big, tan animal sprung out of the water.
"Booo!" it said.
Lars quickly ran to hide.

"I was only joking," called the big, tan animal.
"I'm Henry, the hippopotamus. Who are you and why
are you so white?"

Lars didn't know the answer to the last question.
"Where I come from, everything is white," he said.

He told Henry about his long journey and asked him how he could get back to his father.

Henry listened sympathetically, but be seemed confused. He wiggled his ears and squirmed and finally said, "The only one who can help you is Marcus, the eagle. He has travelled all over the world. He will know where you come from and how you can get back there. But we'll have to cross the river, go through the jungle, and climb the mountains to reach him.'"

Lars was happy to go, but when he looked at the river he said, "The only problem is that I can't swim very well yet."

"No problem at all," said Henry and laughed. "Climb on my back. I won't sink."

Lars was astonished by all the things he saw in the jungle. Henry patiently explained everything. Lars especially liked the tall, brown stalks that Henry called trees. They were such fun to climb!

In one brown stalk sat a funny green animal, which suddenly turned white, just like Lars.

"It's a chameleon," Henry said. "It can change its color."

Lars thought that was a handy thing to be able to do.

At the edge of the jungle, the mountains began. It was a bit cooler and Lars felt more comfortable. Henry found climbing difficult, but Lars helped by telling him where to step.

After a while Henry was exhausted.

"That's enough for today," he said. "Tomorrow we will continue. Let's rest here and look at the nice view."

As Lars looked out over the land and sea, he began to feel homesick.

"Cheer up," said Henry. "You'll be home again soon."

The next day they climbed higher. Henry had to stop
often to catch his breath. But at last he called, "Here
comes Marcus!" as a huge bird swooped down near Lars.
Lars ducked.

"Don't be afraid," said Henry. "Marcus seems gruff,
but he's really quite friendly."

Henry said good morning to Marcus and politely explained why they had come.

The eagle looked at Lars and then said, "Well, well, a polar bear in the tropics! You're a long way from home aren't you, young man? Fortunately I can arrange your passage back. Tomorrow morning I will have Samson fetch you from the beach."

"Thank you very much, sir," Lars said shyly.

The next morning Henry and Lars met Marcus on
the beach. "Right on time," said Marcus proudly as a huge
gray whale arrived.

Although Henry was happy for Lars, he was also sorry
to see him go. "Take care of yourself," he said sadly.

"Thanks for everything, Henry," Lars called as the
whale swam away. Marcus flew along a bit to set them
on their way.

Henry stood alone on the beach. He kept watching for a long time after Lars and the whale had disappeared.

Samson swam a long way until they were surrounded
by ice and snow.

"We must be near your home now," he said.

At the same moment Lars called, "There he is, my
father! Father! I'm back!"

Lars's father couldn't believe his eyes. There was Lars
riding on top of a whale.

Lars's father was very tired from looking for Lars.
But he wasn't too tired to catch a big fish for Samson to
thank him. Samson waved as he swam away.

"And now," said Lars's father, "we must go straight home
because your mother is very worried."

On the way home Lars rode on his father's back. Everything was white and he was surrounded by snow and ice. But this time Lars talked and talked while his father was silent. He told his father about all the amazing things he had seen: Henry, the tall, brown stalks, Marcus, and much more.

"You didn't meet anyone who was white?" asked his father in surprise.

"Nobody, except a chameleon," said Lars, "but that doesn't count."

Lars had to laugh by himself because his father didn't understand his joke.